KT-379-752

Sticker Dolly Dressing
Holiday

Lucy Bowman

Illustrated by Vici Leyhane,
Stella Baggott and Molly Sage

Contents

The stickers fit on any of the dolls, so you can choose what they wear. The back cover folds out so you can "park" spare stickers there while you dress the dolls.

Meet the girls

Chloé, Megan and Tia are at the airport, waiting to board a plane and jet off. They love visiting exciting new places...

Chloé likes shopping and looking her best wherever she is in the world.

Megan loves sightseeing, and enjoys taking photos of all the places she visits.

Tia is sporty, adventurous and fun-loving. She always likes to be on the go.

Tropical beach

On a beautiful tropical island, the girls relax on the golden sand, and swim and surf in the warm blue ocean. When it gets too hot, they eat delicious ice-cream cones to cool down.

Skiing

In the snowy mountains, Megan, Chloé and Tia wrap up in layers of clothes to keep out the icy wind. After warming cups of hot chocolate at a lodge, the girls are ready for action. Tia can't wait to jump onto her snowboard and swoosh down the slopes!

On safari

The girls are on a safari adventure. They've been driving over the African grasslands all morning and have spotted some amazing animals, including elephants, rhinos and zebras. Megan is very excited, as she's managed to take a photo of a cheetah in a tree.

Coral reef

Tia, Megan and Chloé have dived down into the magical world of a coral reef, filled with strange-shaped corals and underwater creatures. They've discovered scuttling crabs, lots of fish, pretty shells and even a giant green turtle.

Taking photos

Megan is visiting the pyramids. It's a scorching hot day, so she wears long loose clothes to keep cool. She takes photos of the pyramids and a camel train as it treks across the sandy desert.

City shopping

Chloé is shopping for clothes in New York. The department stores have all the latest fashions. There's so much to choose from that she already has lots of bags to carry.

All aboard

It's a sunny day and there's a warm breeze blowing across the bay. Chloé, Tia and Megan are getting ready to set sail and join the dolphins splashing around in the clear blue water.

Mermaid

On the ranch

Down on the ranch, Chloé is about to saddle up and go for a ride across the grassy plains, while Tia and Megan are helping to feed the horses. After that, they're going to learn how to use a rope to lasso the cattle — soon they'll be real cowgirls!

Camping out

The girls have found a pretty place to pitch their tents at a campsite. They will spend the day swimming in the lake and watching the birds in the trees, before tucking in for the night in their warm sleeping bags.

Visiting Venice

When it's carnival time in Venice, everyone wears mysterious masks and glamorous gowns. As fireworks light up the night sky, the girls wait for gondolas to take them across the lagoon.

In the jungle

It's hot and humid in the rainforest. The air is filled with the strange noises of monkey calls and bird songs. The girls are excited about exploring the lush jungle, and looking for amazing insects and animals hiding among the plants and trees.

Photo album

After their trips, the girls look through all their photos. They put them in an album so they'll never forget all the amazing places they've visited.

Edited by Leonie Pratt. Series editor: Fiona Watt. This edition first published in 2015 by Usborne Publishing Ltd., 83-85 Saffron Hill, London, EC1N 8RT, England www.usborne.com
Copyright © 2015, 2009 Usborne Publishing Ltd. The name Usborne and the devices ♀ ⊕ are Trade Marks of Usborne Publishing Ltd. All rights reserved. No part of this publication may be reproduced, stored in a retrieval system, or transmitted in any form or by any means, electronic, mechanical, photocopy, recording or otherwise, without prior permission of the publisher. First published in America in 2015. U.E. Printed in Malaysia.

Tropical beach

Pages 4-5

Skiing

coral reef

All aboard

On the ranch

Pages 16-17

camping out

In the jungle

Pages 22-23

Photo album

* Tia by the sea *

* Chloé camping *

* Megan at the pyramids *

Page 24